ONE MISTAKE, RELENTLESS PAIN

A True Story Detailing the Consequences
of Drinking and Driving

DAVID KOCH

TATE PUBLISHING
AND ENTERPRISES, LLC

One Mistake, Relentless Pain
Copyright © 2014 by David Koch. All rights reserved.

The opinions expressed by the author are not necessarily those of Tate Publishing, LLC.

Published by Tate Publishing & Enterprises, LLC
127 E. Trade Center Terrace | Mustang, Oklahoma 73064 USA
1.888.361.9473 | www.tatepublishing.com

Tate Publishing is committed to excellence in the publishing industry. The company reflects the philosophy established by the founders, based on Psalm 68:11,
"The Lord gave the word and great was the company of those who published it."

Book design copyright © 2014 by Tate Publishing, LLC. All rights reserved.

Published in the United States of America

ISBN: 978-1-63185-133-9
1. Self-Help / General
2. Education / Driver Education
01.14.17

A real-life story

of how an executive of a Fortune 50 company
went from a potential promotion opportunity
to being fired within weeks for driving under
the influence of alcohol.

Choices

We make them every day.
My choice was to drink
and get behind the wheel of a car.
Here is my story.
This is what happens when you choose wrong.

Acknowledgments

Thank you to everyone who has supported me during this incredibly challenging, emotional, and financially draining chapter in my life. It is easy to stay positive and upbeat when times are good, not as convenient when they are not. I am grateful for the friends and family who have stood by and with me throughout this ordeal, which can best be described as a continuous cascade of nightmares: Jason Bottiglieri, Jeff Murdock, Jeffrey Tritt, Jack Darby, Todd Lutes, Joe Arico, Ron Resha, Manny Asser, Larry Bitterman, Steve McDaniels, Gregg Jackson, and the entire Arbor Books team.

I would like to extend special thanks to David Gross, probably the one most responsible for helping me maintain my sanity and for countless hours of editing, suggestions, and insights.

To Bob Castellini, who has supported me from day one and is a constant beacon of light for me.

To my parents, who, through their wisdom and love, have always been there for me, even when times were the most challenging.

And to my wife and kids, to whom I am forever grateful for their undeserved patience, support, and love. Through thick and thin was what my wife and I vowed more than twenty years ago. You are about to read a clear example of what "thin" can mean.

A Message from the Author

Thank you for taking the time to read my story and hopefully digest its important message. It is obviously not one that I am proud of, but I am confident it will help you avoid the pain and consequences that will happen if you make the same mistake I did. I try to explain the consequences and nightmare that accompany a DUI in real-life terms.

I worked hard in the medical-device field for more than twenty two years. I was an accomplished sales rep, division manager, and director of marketing for two different Fortune 50 companies. I had built a career that I thought was pretty solid.

I have been married to a wonderful wife for more than twenty years and have eleven-year-old twins who are just perfect, and I have always tried to make the right decisions. I had never been in trouble with the law.

I made a mistake that cost me my career and caused incredible pain to my family and friends.

My story is about the consequences and real-life pain that follow when your luck runs out. The simple goal is to describe in detail what you can expect if you choose to drink and drive. It is a firsthand account of what happens when you choose wrong. You don't want to roll the dice and lose. It is simply not worth it. When you read the story, you will see why.

Two to three drinks can put someone over the legal limit, and there even is a movement in Congress today to lower the acceptable blood alcohol level. In one survey, 30 percent of people admitted to driving under the influence of alcohol within the past year. Does that number seem low to you? It may be because most people think that if they can walk, they are not under the influence. Most people just don't realize the intense sensitivity around drinking and driving and the cascade of hardship that comes with being uninformed. Every time you have a few beers, glasses of wine, or cocktails or any combination of the three and then drive, you are taking an enormous risk that can disrupt your life in more ways than you can imagine.

One and a half million people are arrested each year for DUI. All of them wish they had made a better choice.

I sincerely hope you take the time to read this story and then, more importantly, remember it the next time you find yourself considering taking the risk that could and eventually will turn your life and career upside down.

The Beginning

Have you ever thought about how lucky you are? Have you ever thought about how your life can go sideways in a split second based on one decision? This is the story of how I took everything for granted and made a bad choice. My life, filled with promise, turned into a nightmare.

Our culture revolves around alcohol in many ways. While there are plenty of people who are cognizant of the tolerated limit, many are not. I was one of them.

I made a bad choice. The goal of this story is to detail the cascade of nightmares that followed, in the hope that you don't make the same choice that I made.

Here's Why....

As a senior leader of a Fortune 50 company, I used to stand up in front of organizations and talk about market strategy, lead breakout groups, discuss ways to drive sales, and coach sales forces on how to maximize their potential and make more money. I was a successful sales rep, sales trainer, division manager, and director of marketing. I had it going on. I was on the fast track. I had done all the right things: worked hard, managed my managers well, and had eighteen years of tenure and more than twenty-two years in the medical business space. I was a top candidate for a promotion that would have placed me on the board of my company, which was a big deal. It was the next step up the corporate ladder.

Today I am humbled and embarrassed. But now I have a more important objective than a corporate futures presentation or delivering a marketing strategy slide deck. It's more important than any sales pep talk to my team. I am here to save you from the pain I have endured based on ONE mistake. A mistake that could have easily been avoided. A mistake I own and for which I have paid dearly. A mistake that has affected my entire family and close friends in more ways than I can count.

I made the dumbest choice of my life: I chose to get behind the wheel of my car after drinking too much. I got into an accident at a stoplight and was arrested for driving while under the influence. My choice resulted in a cascade of hardships for so many people—obviously me, but more importantly my wife, family, close friends, colleagues, and the list goes on. The possible resulting hardships never entered my mind when I got into the car. I had heard about how dangerous drinking and driving is a million times. I had heard how the legal system is really cracking down on offenders. I probably had even commented to friends and family about how the courts should throw the book at people who get busted for

DUI. But for some reason, I didn't think it applied to or could possibly happen to me.

I am not a preacher. I am not a motivational speaker, and I am certainly not a saint. I am here to educate you specifically on everything that could someday happen to you if you drink and drive.

My objective is to tell my story about this big mistake with the hope that you don't have to tell yours one day.

I rolled the dice and lost. I gambled thinking the odds were in my favor. Had I known then what I know now, I would have realized the upside was nowhere near the downside.

Drinking and driving can harm and kill innocent people. We've all seen videos and testimonials from both victims and those who caused the harm. We've all heard countless stories and seen graphic pictures of the physical carnage and loss of life and limb when someone loses control of a vehicle because they had too much to drink. The pain it causes families and loved ones is unimaginable. Severe DUI accidents happen every day. Tragically there are habitual offenders.

I am not here to speak about the horrors of killing or hurting someone because of drinking and driving. I thank God every day that didn't happen to me, **but it could have**. My objective is not to show you pictures of mangled cars and huge accidents resulting from someone drinking and driving. Most of us have those etched in our brains from driver-training classes and what we see on the news almost every night. Unfortunately too many of us look at those pictures and subconsciously assume it will not happen to us. That only happens to wild kids or complete boozehounds.

I am here to walk you through exactly what happens if you make the mistake I did. Again, it's something I never thought would happen to me. I made a choice that changed my life and my career. When I get through describing what happened and the subsequent result, you will see why I chose to tell you my story with the hope that you digest it, think about it and make the smart decision I wish I had made.

The Story

On June 25, 2012, I flew from my home in South Florida to New Jersey fully prepared to take on a battery of interviews for a board-level position at a Fortune 50 medical-device company. I was ready to go. Résumé was tight, career summary was intact, 30/60/90-day plan looked good. Checked in to a local hotel by the corporate office and got a solid night's sleep. In my mind the job was mine to lose.

The next day the interviews went great. I felt really good leaving the multitude of interviews you have to go through when you are in the running for a senior leadership position. Before it's over, everybody and their brother needs to weigh in on it. I was completely burned out, but I was really optimistic. All signs were pointed my way for the job. In my mind my biggest concern was that I would have to sell my wife and kids on moving to New Jersey and leaving sunny Florida. I figured I had the job locked.

> *Here is where judgment comes into play. Here is the fork in the road where a poor decision can disrupt your life in more ways than you can imagine.*

Not knowing how long the interviews would last, I wanted to be safe with my flight times, so I booked a flight out of Newark at 8:00 p.m. My interviews were done at about three o'clock. After making the rounds in the main office, talking to friends, etc., I jumped into my rental car and headed to the airport.

I had time. For some reason I decided to stop, grab a late lunch, and drink before returning my rental car at the airport. Maybe it was to kill some time or to relieve some stress and call some of my friends to let them know how well it had gone. It doesn't really matter. What does matter is I chose to drink. I chose to drink and then drive. At the time I was thinking about two things: relocation

1

to New Jersey and helping my family feel comfortable with the move. Why did I drink and get behind the wheel of a car? Why would I jeopardize everything over a few cocktails? Why didn't I think about the consequences?

I don't know. What I do know is that I didn't understand the ramifications of my choice until the next morning and the days to come. I had no idea what would happen if I was arrested for driving under the influence. It never entered my mind.

Every one of us has been challenged with decisions like this. Every one of us has rolled the dice. Chances are you have been lucky so far. If you are reading this right now and have been behind the wheel after having a few too many drinks, trust me, you have been lucky. But you don't want to press that luck. Let me say that again: you don't ever want to press that luck.

Here's what happens when your luck runs out.

JAIL

I was driving to the airport in my rental car, and because I was not familiar with the area, I began trying to use the navigation system in the car, which meant I took my eyes off the road. Couple that with my slow reaction speed due to the alcohol, and the result was me rear-ending another car at an intersection. I didn't see the light change and obviously was not able to avoid the car in front of me. I could have killed someone.

I was arrested and processed. Based on what the police officer told me, New Jersey mandates a minimum of twelve hours in the county jail if you do not have someone available to pick you up. I didn't. Let me tell you, the county jail is no Marriott. It was a seven-by-seven cell with a plastic mattress and no blankets or pillows. It was dank and cold and, to be polite, my neighbors were not necessarily people I would prefer to have as my neighbors. Twelve hours is a long time when you are trapped in a dungeon.

The guard was kind enough to deliver an inedible sandwich

and a cup of black coffee at one point during the night. I was released around noon the next day due to processing delays. I had been a prisoner for roughly sixteen hours in total. Think about that: Sixteen hours in a holding cell. No information about when I was going to be released or my fate. Throughout the evening I had to use all of my energy simply to relax. My heart was racing, and my anxiety level was enormous.

Remember the last time you were stuck in traffic? Dead stop. Feeling trapped. No exits, no lane changes, and no way out. Maybe it lasted for ten minutes or maybe for an hour. You knew you'd get out eventually, but it didn't help your stress level. One night in a cell is like that times one hundred. My freedom was gone. I was not allowed to do anything but lie on the ratty plastic bed and wait… and wait…and wait…. I think I even counted the ceiling tiles a few times.

They took my shoes because they had laces. They took my belt and all other personal items. I couldn't be trusted. I was officially a criminal in custody. There was no distinction between me and the guy in the next cell, who was allegedly in for armed robbery. I heard cell doors opening and shutting all night. I heard loud voices and guys pleading for leniency. I heard officers talking to everyone like they were the scum of the earth. At that point we all were. No freedom, little dignity, and at the complete mercy of someone and something else. The judicial system was about to come slamming down on me. One mistake, one terrible decision. Welcome to hell.

When I was released, an officer returned my personal items. The clerk behind the bulletproof glass was kind enough to call a cab to drive me to the towing lot where my rental car was. I needed to get my luggage and phone. The attendant at the tow station walked me around the building to show me where my rental car was parked. The sight of the car the next day made the hair stand up on my arms. I knew it was un-drivable with the front end smashed in to the point where it was half its original size. I knew both airbags had also been deployed, but seeing it the next day and imagining the worst that could have happened was both terrifying and sobering. It is hard to describe the emotion that was draped over me. Standing in that parking lot, holding my luggage and looking at the car, was one of the worst moments of my life. I had been in a cell for sixteen hours. I was disheveled, anxious, and dirty. How had this happened? Since the cab had already left, I now had to call another cab to drive me to the airport, leaving behind a bashed and broken rental car. I immediately called the rental company to let them know their car was undrivable. I bet you can guess the time and paperwork that were soon to come.

Talk about a drive of shame. My wife was calling. My colleagues and friends were calling. What was I going to say? How was I going to explain this? I had a feeling I was screwed in a variety of ways. Guess what? I was. More than I ever could have imagined.

A cascade of nightmares ensues.

MY JOB

Instead of being the top candidate for a promotion to lead a senior-level team, sit on the board of a Fortune 50 company, and advance my career, I was released (otherwise known as "fired") for a "class-one violation." What I've learned the hard way is that most companies have strict conduct policies, especially relating to drinking and driving. Most organizations have zero tolerance. I didn't know or think those rules applied to me. I called my company and told them everything. I guess I thought my tenure and credentials would help me get through this. I was wrong.

I received a text from my boss soon after the arrest suggesting we "catch up on some business issues." He gave me a conference-call number and a time. I didn't think it was a big deal but was curious: why a conference call? Why not just call me from his cell?

When I called in, we chatted for a few minutes about his recent vacation, and then I suggested we save a few dollars and just talk via cell. Here is how the conversation went from there:

My manager: We are going to be joined by HR, which is why we are on this call.

A representative from HR then identified himself as having joined the call.

HR: We cannot overlook your actions. Being arrested for driving under the influence is a class-one violation of our policies. As a result you are being terminated effective immediately.

No warning, no consideration of my résumé or my eighteen-year tenure with the company. There was no waiting to see if I had actually been convicted. I was angry and confused and felt betrayed by the company I had dedicated myself to for eighteen years.

However, time cleared my head. It was my decision to drink and drive that car. It was my decision. It wasn't the fault of the people to whom I reported. It wasn't human resources'. It was my fault. I made the decision. I had to own it. Their hands were tied. It took me about twelve months to get that.

In retrospect I wish it had dawned on me to actually read the alcohol-related sections of my employer's handbook. You know—the small print none of us ever actually reads until we're blindsided by that tiny clause that leaves us powerless. Alcohol is pervasive in the corporate culture. It is part of every corporate function and most personal outings like dinners, ball games, concerts, and family cookouts for that matter. Why would I not know my company's stance? Why would I take the risk? I ask myself that daily. Again, my goal is to help you avoid those same questions.

After being let go, the hassles—not to mention the financial element that came with it—were enormous. When you think about all the things you take for granted when you have a solid job, the list gets long. And when you wake up the day after being fired, you have a lot of things to consider. Here are a few of the big ones:

How do you explain it to family and friends?

Most people try to be supportive, but in the back of your mind you know they're probably thinking about how you just wasted your career. My wife refuses to tell her friends and her immediate family to this day. She is too embarrassed. I have told close friends but am selective only because word travels fast. My situation is not something I want or need to travel fast.

My parents, older brother, and younger sister have been supportive. It kind of goes with the territory. My in-laws would not be as supportive. I have not told my eleven-year-old kids. I am too embarrassed, and there is no reason to expose them to this kind of situation yet. I plan to wait until they are older and use this as an example of something they need to avoid.

What do you do for medical, dental, and life insurance for the family that relies on you?

Private health insurance for a family of four is about $1,800 per month. The application process is arduous to say the least. Even though most plans are designed to continue similar coverage by the same carrier you had while you were employed, the paperwork that needs to be completed takes hours. I am now a high-risk customer, so the required paperwork is doubled and so are the costs of coverage.

I was also denied life insurance coverage because I was high-risk due to the DUI.

What do you do with your 401(k)? Where do you put your money?

That conversion process can also be arduous and time-consuming. Otherwise known as a pain in the "bleep." First I had to find an investment advisor. Before the accident all of that had been taken care of by my employer. Then I had to determine an investment strategy, fill out more paperwork, and go through the process of transferring everything over. More time, more hassles and uncertainty.

When I left my company, I had no income, but I had bills.

Unfortunately those don't go away with a loss of income. I had to reach into my retirement savings to bridge the time between jobs. Call it being naïve, call it another stupid move, but I did not take out the taxes upfront. As a result I just received an enormous tax bill and will need to dip into my depleting savings once again to pay it. More stress, more hardship, more pain.

As a nice little side note, I lost a significant amount of unexercised stock options the day I was fired.

No company car. I had to buy a car. More time. More hassle. More headaches.

Instead of a car that is fully paid for, I now have to pay for it myself. Car payment, insurance, maintenance, gas. Obviously most people deal with this every day, but I had had the benefit of driving a company vehicle for more than twenty-two years.

I should have waited to purchase a new car though, because I have no use for it now (for reasons I'll get to later). I have the nicest unused, un-drivable car in the neighborhood. At least I'm not putting any miles on it.

By the way, based on my personal experience, if you are not eliminated from the policy altogether, car insurance costs go up roughly $7,000 per year if you are charged with a DUI. The additional premium was painful enough. One year after the arrest, because I was now "high risk," my car insurance company cancelled my policy. Not just for me but for my wife as well. They said it is their policy that when one driver in a household has his or her license revoked, all drivers in that household are included in their decision. My wife was the one who opened the letter from the insurance company. She was not happy.

You turn in all of your company assets.

My computer was shut off from the home office on the day I was fired, and I lost all of my files. The computer was locked. The password to log in was no longer valid. I had used my company laptop for both work and personal things. It was where I stored everything. Even my company of eighteen years didn't trust me.

My cell phone was turned off. I had to go buy a new one. I lost all my data and had to change my phone number. That meant I had to let all my friends, colleagues, family, creditors, etc. know about both the change in the number and the reason for it. More time and hassle.

What kind of job can you pursue with not only a firing but a felony on your record?

You are ultimately limited to smaller, startup type companies—if you're lucky enough to find something suitable in the right part of the country. Good luck with that these days.

Larger companies do extensive background checks on both your criminal and driving records. You will have a zero-percent chance of getting through that even if you are the right candidate and do well throughout the interview process.

I was a lead candidate (per my recruiter) for a great job based in Florida. We had a final interview set up with the final decision maker. Good money, benefits, and local to where I live now. Then the phone stopped ringing. They clearly did a background check, saw I had a DUI on my record, and lost interest. Game over.

So, I've listed just a few of the hassles and headaches from a career perspective that happen when you are fired for a class-one violation. There are so many more. So many little things that add up. So many things you may or may not take for granted. Every day for the last twelve months, I have run into another hassle that chips away at my core. Every day something new pops up that makes me slump over in my chair and shake my head.

Every day I ask myself why I was so stupid and unaware.

Just as important, from an emotional standpoint, are the fear, uncertainty, and stress that just can't be measured and are really difficult to explain. One day you are immersed in your work; you have a solid routine, clear objectives, and a plan to succeed. The next day you find yourself staring at an empty desk, a blank calendar, and a future that is unknown, which makes it horrifying.

Emotionally trying to handle everything going on—the changes, the responsibilities, and what the future holds coupled with the day-to-day tactical management of the situation—is more challenging and heart-wrenching than I can put into words. Again, trust me: you don't want to experience it.

> *The pain of my choice to get behind the wheel of that car after drinking too much was just getting started.*

FINDING AN ATTORNEY

The first thing I had to do was find a lawyer in New Jersey to represent me, help me navigate the legal system and help me avoid the harshest penalties. The harshest of all was jail time followed by an extended loss of license, felony charges on my record, and massive fines.

A previous colleague recommended an attorney based in New Jersey who was experienced with DUI defense, so we connected and scheduled an initial meeting at his office. A thousand dollars later (after flights, hotel, cabs, parking, etc.), we discussed an action plan, which of course included my having to come up with $2,500 (from my quickly diminishing savings) for his services. That turned out to be just a down payment.

My attorney knew what he was doing, but he did not have much of a bedside manner. He was not the type of lawyer who makes you feel warm and fuzzy about the situation. He actually took it to the opposite extreme, painting a picture that made my stomach turn and sweat form on my forehead. I was hoping he would tell me everything would be just fine, like, "This is your first offense. I've got you covered." Instead he said things like, "I'm just trying to keep you out of jail." This only added to my already off-the-charts stress level. He dealt with this kind of situation daily. All he was doing was setting realistic expectations. He made it perfectly clear that this was serious.

But "just trying to keep me out of jail?" Let that marinate for a few seconds. I was forty-five years old, had been an upstanding citizen and taxpayer my entire adult life, and had eleven-year-old twins and a wife at home. I'd never been in trouble with the law. I'd just lost my job of eighteen years. And now jail was a possibility? What the "bleep" was going on? Trust me when I tell you my trip back to Florida was one I would like to forget. The ensuing months were something that I would like to delete from my memory bank altogether.

The legal system and the government do not function like a business. Everything takes forever. I was arrested in June. I met with my attorney in early July. I finally got a call from him in August with bad news. I had cut him a check for $2,500 then had to wait and stress out for two months for a simple update, and that update was bad news?

Because I had caused an accident at a stoplight accompanied by a DUI, the prosecutor decided he was going to charge me with a criminal felony—reckless driving, driving while under the influence, assault with an automobile, and a few other throw-ins. He was going to move the case from the county courthouse (where charges and punishments were less severe) to the state courthouse. Not good. In fact it could not have been worse. Even though I had been a good citizen, my decision to get behind the wheel after too many drinks took me out of the "good citizen" line and placed me right in the middle of the "derelict" line.

I was a designated dirt bag in the eyes of the prosecutor.

Because we were now going to big-boy court, if I wanted to retain my current attorney, his additional fee was $5,000. If the case went to trial, his fee was $2,500 per day on top of that. I spent the next few days researching other attorneys, talking to people I knew and ultimately, after an exhaustive search, I decided to stay with my current attorney. He, it turned out, knew the area, the people, and the process as well as anyone. And he was already engaged in the case.

Sound like fun so far?

Being a seasoned attorney, the first thing he told me to do was to check into an outpatient rehabilitation facility immediately. I needed to be proactive in showing the court I had addressed my alcohol issue and was serious about not repeating the same mistake in the future. Did I need treatment? Did I need to check in to a facility to get help? It didn't matter. If I was going to minimize the damage and perhaps stay out of jail, I was going to rehab. It wasn't even an option. Because of my actions and bad judgment, I didn't fight it.

The next giant chunk of my time was all about finding a facility that worked with my schedule. I had found another job as a consultant for a startup medical company. It was just a ninety-day contract, but at least I had income. They were so small they didn't do background checks. Thankfully they were flexible, which I needed for obvious reasons. I landed at a health-and-wellness center about forty-five minutes from my house. It was far away from my house and a hassle to get to and from, but I had no choice.

This was after visiting some really bad places. The county facility (which was cheapest) housed primarily crack addicts, heroin abusers, habitual DUIs, and the homeless. I spent six hours in that facility, meeting with doctors and staff and being processed, before finally getting up and running out of there as fast as I could. I visited a few others, most of which required inpatient treatment, before landing at the center that met my needs.

I spent three months at the center, initially all day every day but then cutting it back to a couple times per week. The program was intense. It included everything from exercise classes, yoga, and group meetings to private therapy sessions. It was a complete health-and-wellness center. I would show up at the small campus and get a printed schedule showing me which appointment was where and when. Completing the program was mandatory.

The most significant downside? It cost close to $13,000 out of my pocket. That hurt big time. What is also important to point out is that I had lost my options for where and when I had to be somewhere. I couldn't do what I wanted to do. It felt like my freedom was in the hands of someone else. It was not a nice feeling.

So then it was January, coming up on seven months after the arrest, and I didn't have a court date yet. I'd just gone through the holidays with family and friends. My wife and I had chosen to tell only a select group of people about what was going on. Call it embarrassment coupled with simply wanting to talk about something else. Do you know how challenging it is to selectively tell one person one thing and something different to someone else? I'm not talking about lying. I'm talking about remembering what you have divulged about a situation and to whom and when.

PRE-INTERVENTION TRIAL PROGRAM

I finally got a bit of good news in February, eight months after my arrest. After paying my attorney $7,500 and all the travel costs, he was able to convince the district attorney to allow me to interview for acceptance into the PTI (Pre-Trial Intervention) Program of New Jersey. Can you see the irony in that? The last time I had been in New Jersey for an interview, I had been thrown in jail. Now I was going back, this time interviewing to stay out of jail.

This program was designed for first-time DUI offenders. If accepted into the program, as explained to me, I would pay a fine, do community service work for a nonprofit organization and be put on probation for roughly a year. If I met the requirements at the end of the program, my record would be expunged. It would be clean. My attorney thought it was great news and, for the first time, I sensed optimism in his voice.

I would have to fly back to New Jersey, get a hotel, pay for a cab and everything else that came with the trip, and then spend an entire day at the state courthouse pleading to get into the program. First I had to register in one building, pay a $75 fee and then bring the paperwork to another building. February in New Jersey can be a little chilly. It was snowing sideways. Being used to Florida weather, I was miserable.

I then waited the rest of the morning for my appointment with the PTI officer. My anxiety level was at an all-time high at that point. If I got accepted into the program, at least the pain would be reduced. If I didn't get accepted, I'd be in big trouble. You don't want to feel the way I felt that day emotionally. Top it with where and with whom I spent it and you have an all-time crappy day. Trust me on that. I spent at least two hours with the PTI officer talking about the arrest, my job, my family, my life. She wanted to find out if I was worthy of avoiding valuable court time. It was like I was on the most important sales call or interview of my life. The big difference was that if I failed, I didn't just lose a sale, I'd be screwed on multiple levels. Those two days up and back to New Jersey were another two days I want to forget. Stress, fear of the unknown, and then throw in running around courthouses, waiting…waiting… waiting. I was so glad to get on the plane and go home.

My attorney called me the next week with the good news that I had been accepted into the PTI program. I had passed the test. Now it was going to be up to the judge to accept the application and determine the specific punishment. At the time I was pumped up. I could see light at the end of the tunnel. This nightmare was coming to an end. I had endured enough. All that was left was to stand before the judge, process the paperwork, and fulfill my obligations for the PTI program. I could then move on with my life.

Not so fast….

THE COURT DATE

That's right: another trip to New Jersey. Same movie, different day. I flew from Fort Lauderdale to Newark the day before my appearance date to stand before the judge at the Mercer County Courthouse. Hotel, cab, and expenses totaling more than $1,000. The cost hurt, but getting to the courthouse at 8:00 a.m. and sitting in the hallway for hours alongside drug dealers and other repeat felons was the most painful. Based on my eavesdropping, most had been there before, and what struck me was they didn't really seem to care. I did.

Finally the judge would hear our case. Two hours and seemingly a ton of paperwork later, I was able to interact with him. He did not treat me like a senior-level executive. He did not treat me as if I had done all the right things in my life and made one mistake. He didn't treat me any differently from the people involved in the last few cases I had observed. He treated me like a moron. He treated and spoke to me as if I were a criminal.

Guess what? I was. I was humiliated, and the more I thought about it, the more angry I got at myself. I had put myself in this spot. I had done it. I had made that choice. If I had known then what I know now....

So once the case was heard and the banter between my attorney and the prosecutor concluded, the judge officially accepted my application for the PTI program. Twelve months of probation, checking in with the probation officer monthly, forty hours of community service work, fines of about $700, and loss of driving privileges in New Jersey for six months. I also was required to continue substance abuse treatment for twelve months. I'm not asking for sympathy, but are you personalizing this yet?

One mistake. One bad decision....

After my court appearance, I had to go down to the basement of the courthouse to introduce myself to the probation officer, fill out more paperwork, and try to learn what was expected of me, what I had to do, and the general rules. Again I had the pleasure of sitting in a waiting room filled with people who had committed far worse crimes than I had. Let me tell you, they don't have a separate waiting area for those wearing suits. You can't pass the clerk a ten spot and get to the front of the line. If you are in that room, you are a dirt bag—period.

My attorney had slapped me a high-five while going down to the probation office in the elevator, happy that I was able to keep my Florida license and then had to take off. His job was over. "All you have to do now is fill out some paperwork. No big deal." I just said thanks.

After organizing the reams of paper and outlining the requirements and rules I had to follow over the next twelve months, I had to run through the snow to get back to my hotel, hoping they would grant me a late checkout, so I wouldn't have to pay for another night. While running through the streets like a wild man, I was calling the airline to get on a flight that day. I was tired and felt dirty, stressed, and partially panicked. I had been given a million instructions, dates, and tasks. I just wanted to get the hell out of New Jersey and see my family.

Here is just one set of instructions—the standard provisions of PTI supervision:

- You shall obey all federal, state, and municipal ordinances. You shall notify your probation officer within twenty-four hours if you are arrested or issued a complaint summons in any jurisdiction.
- You shall report to your probation officer as directed.
- You shall answer all inquiries by your probation officer truthfully.
- You shall permit your probation officer to visit your residence or any other suitable place.
- You shall promptly report any change of address or residence to your probation officer.
- You must obtain permission if you wish to move outside the state.
- You shall seek and maintain gainful employment and promptly notify your probation officer when you change your employment or find yourself out of work.
- You shall cooperate in any test, treatment, and/or counseling deemed necessary by your probation officer during the PTI period of postponement.

Still sound like a good time?

This was the program I so highly coveted. This was the good stuff. If I had not gone to New Jersey twice, spent multiple days in the courthouse, hired an attorney, and dealt with the mounting expenses, my situation and life would have been even worse. I got off easy.

What's next?

It was the middle of March 2013, eight months after the arrest and three months after my consulting contract with the startup company ran out. Income stream gone. Basic things I used to expense, like phone, car, office supplies, postage…gone. What were my options? My only option was to work for myself because there were no companies that would touch someone who had a DUI on their record. I started writing this book to keep busy and try to make some sense of it all.

The true reality in the eyes of any company:
"You have lack of judgment, control, and willpower.
Game over, thanks for playing.

Last year, prior to the arrest, I was called by probably twenty recruiters hoping to see if I had interest in a career change. Many were nice opportunities. I said no to all of them. I was comfortable and secure. My future was great. The calls still come today, but I don't even pick up the phone. I know it's a waste of everyone's time. The second a company pulls my record, I'm done. My only option for the next twelve months at minimum is to work independently because I can hire myself.

The first thing I had to do was connect with my probation officer in New Jersey. Our scheduled phone appointment was delayed because of the storms, floods, and power outages in the area at that time. We finally connected and she, although nice on the phone, didn't care about me or my situation. I was one of hundreds of criminals she worked with. I was no different. She explained to me what my obligations were to the court and to her.

It was confusing, complicated, and unorganized. My stress level went up exponentially.

Community service work was a key component of the PTI program. I chose a nonprofit organization that helped to motivate youth and collegiate-level students to support community service and help others. Although my obligation was forty hours, I actually would do more. I think it's a great organization that produces really good results and has the best intentions.

Although I had no income, an inability to expense anything, expensive benefits, and a multitude of other issues having to do with my arrest, I also had to work in forty hours of community service. Time, time, time. I'm thankful I had the opportunity to work for this organization, but I needed to get my own life in order. My wife and family needed me to get back in the game. My stress was rising higher.

Can it get any more painful?

Yes. Probation for twelve months was no big deal. I didn't plan on breaking the law any time soon. I had the community service work set. I found an AA meeting hall I visited weekly not only to comply with PTI but because it helped me clear my head and think through things.

Here is a little add-on: As instructed by the court, I was to contact my probation officer on a monthly basis. I called, faxed, and e-mailed her more than ten times in the first month with no reply. Was she receiving my messages? If I wasn't able to contact my parole officer, would I be considered in violation of the court order? Would it matter that I had made a good-faith effort to contact her? I felt powerless, believing that my future would depend on whether or not someone who barely knew me picked up her telephone.

When I finally did get in touch with her, what surprised me most was how unconcerned she sounded about the matter. I'd left messages—of course I was complying. To her I was simply one of many individuals on probation, one more name to check off a list once a month. But everything that had happened to me since my initial arrest had been a strange, new world to me. I didn't know the rules. I only knew what I'd been told by my lawyer, the judge, and my parole officer. If they couldn't be reached, I had no idea what would happen to me next. As I am writing this, I still have no idea if I am in compliance in the eyes of the NJ court system, and that is all that matters. More stress.

The next issue I didn't see coming….

Do you remember when my attorney was giving me a high-five after the appearance before the judge? He was excited about the fact that I had been accepted into the PTI program and had not lost my license. The ruling was I would lose my driving privileges in New Jersey for six months, but because I had a Florida license, I allegedly was able to drive anywhere but New Jersey. It was the only good news coming out of court that day.

Think again.

In the past states didn't interact like they do now, and there was no federal mandate telling them to do so. Today if you commit a crime (in my case DUI), it is immediately sent to a national registry, and **all** states enforce that ruling. In other words I was not only banned from driving in New Jersey for six months, I was banned from driving anywhere, in any state, for six months. **I didn't get that memo**. Seriously, I did not get the notice from the state of Florida, letting me know that my license was revoked back in March until mid-April. The news was bad enough. The delay in notifying me directly correlates to the next nightmare in my life.

I was sitting in a parking lot in South Florida at about nine in the morning in early-April, talking on the phone, trying to build my business and juggle all the things in my life. It was a beautiful morning. I remember thinking about how great the weather is here in South Florida, but I had a million things going through my head: How was I going to resurrect my career, pay the bills, meet my obligations to the court? I had to speak with my attorney and probation officer. I had to deal with changing my health-care provider, taxes, and life insurance. Twelve months earlier I had been managing a sales team and preparing my résumé for an expected promotion.

Guess what? The story gets worse.

A Broward County sheriff pulled into the parking lot where I was sitting, slowly drove around, and then backed up and placed the nose of his car on the back of mine. My heart and mind were racing; my body was shaking. What the "bleep" was going on? What had I done now, and when was this nightmare going to end?

It is again hard to describe my nerves as I watched the officer open his car door and slowly get out of his cruiser. He adjusted his hat and sauntered up to the rear of my car's window.

The conversation was simple. Here's how it went:

> *Officer: Do you have any weapons in the car?*
> Me: No sir.
> *Officer: What are you doing here?*
> Me: Talking on the phone.
> *Officer: Please get out of the car and lean against your vehicle.*
> Me: Yes sir.
> *Officer: Can I see your license?*
> Me: Here it is.
> *Officer: Do you realize your license is suspended?*
> Me: I had no idea.
> *Officer: Have you been arrested recently?*
> Me: Yes, DUI in New Jersey.

At that point it was clear that he had randomly run my plate and had seen that it was registered to me. The system had immediately alerted him to the fact that the owner of the vehicle had a suspended license. News travels fast apparently.

I went on to explain that when I was in court, there was no mention of my license being suspended or revoked in Florida. It was specifically addressed in the courtroom by the judge. Had I possessed a New Jersey driver's license, they would have taken it. Because I was a Florida resident with a Florida license, they would not take it. I could not drive in New Jersey for six months. That was the message: don't drive in New Jersey for six months.

> *Officer: You were told wrong. You are in the national registry, and all states comply.*
> Me: Holy "bleep." I'm completely "bleeped" now.

My hands and legs were shaking as I was standing eye to eye with him. There were two questions racing through my mind: Would this impact my PTI program? One of the conditions of the program was that I stay out of trouble. If I got into trouble, the deal was off and I would have to fly back to New Jersey and stand before the judge. The second question was: How was I going to explain this to my wife? She was already angry and disappointed in me. Again I was a wreck. I repeat, you don't ever want to be in this spot.

I thought I was toast. Driving with a suspended license is a big deal. If Florida knew about the DUI, New Jersey would certainly know about an arrest for driving with a suspended license. To my great relief, the sheriff was kind enough not to arrest me and throw me in jail, I think because I was polite, truthful, and respectful. He could have arrested me, and he said as much. How about that for a call to my wife? In jail again—got some time to come bail me out? By the way I blew my PTI and might have to fly back to New Jersey and spend some time in jail. Absolute nightmare!

Obviously I wasn't allowed to drive my car home. I could no longer drive anywhere. The sheriff waited for me to call my wife and explain the situation and then for her to come pick up her husband of twenty years in a parking lot, boxed in by a police car. I had to explain to her that even though New Jersey had suspended my license, apparently all states connected and followed suit. I had to try to explain that what I had done had eliminated my right to drive.

The officer wrote me a ticket but not like a parking ticket or speeding ticket. This was a big one. It required me to stand before a judge in Broward County for driving with a suspended license. Even though I had not been driving, my car was off, and the keys were not in the ignition, it didn't matter. What did matter was the headache this whole mess continued to cause.

This was obviously an enormous setback and completely out of the blue. One of the reasons I had hired an attorney in New Jersey was to help me keep my license in Florida, so I could at least function like a normal human being. Today I am trapped in my house unless my wife takes me somewhere or I call a cab. It is much like house arrest. Six months seems like six years.

My next move was to call my attorney in New Jersey, my least-favorite state in the universe at that point, to find out what was going on with the national registry and then to find out what I should do now.. He recommended an attorney in Florida who knew Florida law.

You guessed it: $800 later I had an attorney in Florida who, I hoped, could represent me, help me understand the current laws and help me clear my new record. However, the biggest problem was my license. I couldn't drive for six months. Think about that. I couldn't even drive a scooter (I looked into it).

Because I can be a control freak at times, my kids have never been in the car with their mom and me with their mom behind the wheel. I am the one who drives. When all of a sudden that changed, how could I explain it? Why wasn't Dad driving? Normal questions from eleven-year-olds; nothing but crappy answers from this forty-five-year-old.

I will say it again: you don't want to experience it.

NEW COURT DATE

A new court date was set in Broward County, so I could try to explain why I had no idea my license was suspended in every state. By the way, a few days after being cited for driving with a suspended license in Florida, I received the official legal notice from Florida stating my license was suspended. Why I didn't receive notice of said suspension until days after the county sheriff wrote the citation and almost two months after the New Jersey court date is beyond me. I had literally been driving with a suspended license without knowing it.

My attorney in Florida was able to convince the prosecutor of the misunderstanding, so the felony charge was dropped to a parking ticket and, of course, a fine of $300 payable to the great county of Broward. At that point I was more than willing to cut a check. It did not affect my PTI. I had come so close to magnifying my nightmare. It was almost like someone decided I had endured enough pain for the time being. It was like the difference between stubbing your toe really hard and having your foot cut off.

The bottom line is that it was more stress, time, hardship and all because of one bad decision, one bad mistake. And the hits keep on coming....

THE SAGA CONTINUES

I had dodged a huge bullet. It was June, one full year after being arrested for DUI. Three months after my court appearance in NJ. The good news was that the clock on the PTI program, probation, and reinstatement of my driver's license had been ticking. I felt like I was in the middle of the most boring schoolroom, watching the clock and waiting for the bell to sound. I couldn't wait to get out and breathe the air.

Summer was upon us. The kids were out of school, and family vacation became the topic of conversation. Trying to plan a vacation on a limited budget and with no driver's license was a challenge to say the least. Couple that with my need to manage all of the logistics and requirements of probation and it made for a relatively stressful vacation.

It's a good thing I had a valid passport, because if we wanted to fly somewhere and I didn't have one, we would have been out of luck. I had no license. I carried my passport everywhere in case I needed to show identification. I usually got strange looks when I used it in lieu of a driver's license.

We looked into a rental car for a portion of our vacation, but the company I had used religiously for more than two decades was no longer interested in renting to me. I wonder why....

Do you remember when I mentioned that nearly every day something new comes up that eats away at my core and makes me slump over in my chair? Multiple little things that just rear their ugly heads and burn my time and test my patience.

In July, during my monthly conference call with my probation officer in NJ (four months after the court appearance in NJ), she dropped another bomb on me. My PTI program lasted six months, but unless my lawyer could get an exception through the district attorney's office, my probation was on the books for twenty-four months. Two years until my record (assuming I met all requirements) would be clear and expunged. I wouldn't have a DUI on my record, but for potentially twenty four months, I would have a felony charge pending.

Again, this surprising bit of news, which nobody cared to share with me until nearly five months after the court appearance, will clearly preclude me from working at any major corporation. Background checks will quickly highlight the fact that I have a felony pending. Obviously this was bad news. I was getting used to bad news.

My PTI program concludes in mid-September. One of the last couple of boxes to check are registering and attending a state-run DUI training class and installing an interlock system in my car. The class consists of two consecutive days of six-hour classes followed by a one-hour evaluation. Thirteen hours in a classroom, not to mention a drive time of forty-five minutes each way. Throw in the fact that my wife will need to chauffeur me and that only adds to the hassle and headache. By the way, the cost of the class is $300.

The interlock system is required for all DUI offenders for a minimum of ninety days after license reinstatement. It is a system that has to be installed by the manufacturer and requires the driver of the vehicle to blow into a device and register a zero alcohol level before the car will start. I am not allowed to drive any car that does not have this device installed. It will specifically highlight that when I get my new license.

Another little twist came up when my parole officer mentioned I "might need the physician at the health center to fill out the state form of completion" to document that I officially completed the outpatient program. The letter on his own letterhead, which he wrote at the conclusion of my stay back in January, may not be in the right format! What "might" means to me is that she doesn't know the answer. Based on my experience, I can only assume that I will be immersed in a massive fire drill a day or two before my PTI program ends. So much fun.

I e-mailed the physician at the wellness center to request that he simply fill out the state form, but because it had been nearly nine months since I was a patient (and perhaps because there was no money in it for him), he may require an appointment to "see what he can write." This probably means another trip to the center (forty-five minutes each way) and asking my wife for another ride. Hassle, time, and the stress of the unknown continue to be relentless.

Everything I have described could have been avoided, which makes it that much more painful. Please believe me, you don't want to experience it. You don't have to experience it. You simply need to be aware, think about it before you take the risk, and then make the right choice.

The Least That Could Happen

Before my arrest I never would have imagined the breadth of hardship, pain, and stress that comes with a decision to drink and drive. My story is not unique. Too many people find themselves in similar situations and choose wrong, just like I did. My plight sounds brutal, but in retrospect it could have been much worse. I was lucky.

Let's review the minimum penalties of a DUI in most states. The things that absolutely **will** happen to you if you are convicted of a DUI.

First of all, you will be a convicted felon. Even if you don't serve jail time (which is far from a guarantee), you will at minimum need to report to a parole officer. Your ability to drive, to own a firearm, and to work in certain career fields will be limited. Sometimes (as in my case) these limitations will be temporary **if** you have no prior convictions, **if** you have no history of alcohol-related incidents, **if** you are allowed to participate in something like the PTI program, **if** your state even has something like the PTI program available, **if** you are able to afford a good attorney, and **if** the judge hearing your case doesn't want to make an example of you. So, if you're very lucky, you might just have to reorganize your schedule around a parole officer and a government-mandated program, neither of which are interested in what is convenient for you.

Your insurance rates will go up. You'll notice there are no **ifs** accompanying that statement. It's just a fact. Once you are convicted of a DUI, you will be considered high-risk. And that means more than just higher auto insurance rates. That means higher health-insurance and life-insurance rates as well. And that's assuming your insurance carrier doesn't just drop you completely like mine did.

Finally there is the stigma with employers, friends, coworkers, and even family members. Many people don't differentiate between a habitual drunk driver and someone who got behind the wheel after having too many drinks just once. Even when I get my license back, how many people will think twice before asking me to pick up their kids from soccer practice? How many of my friends know someone who was injured or killed in a drunk-driving accident, and how many of them will project the rage they feel toward that drunk driver onto me? To a lot of people, one drunk driver's the same as any other. And even if my record is expunged and all my legal rights are returned to me and I get another job, those attitudes will never go away.

And I was lucky.

How Could It Have Been Worse?
My lawyer's primary goal was to keep me out of jail. In New Jersey I could have been jailed for up to thirty days. Had I been arrested in Florida, it could have been six to nine months. And, keep in mind, those numbers apply only to first offenses. Repeat offenses, obviously, bring much higher sentences—we're talking years.

And while we're on the subject of repeat offenses, guess how much benefit of the doubt you're going to get if you're involved in another accident, even if you haven't been drinking? My second encounter with a police officer occurred when my car was parked and my crime was simply sitting behind the wheel. After one DUI you will be watched and even if you are technically innocent until proven guilty, the police, the judge and the jury will all be predisposed not to trust you.

My company let me go after the arrest. After the conviction none of the big companies would even speak to me once they ran a background check. I've had some luck with startup companies, but that's only because of the line of work I am in. If I had been a teacher, a day-care worker, a lawyer, or a driver, there would be nowhere for me to go. I'd have to start a whole new career at forty-five, whatever experience I'd built up in my field lost to one conviction.

I mentioned how the level at which states communicate with one another surprised me (and my lawyer). But there is a communication network that's even more pervasive: the Internet. I'm not talking about just my arrest records being available to the public. I'm talking about friends and family just exchanging idle chatter via Facebook, Twitter, or any of the other social media sites. And this is assuming any embarrassing information would get leaked by accident ("oh, I thought you knew why David couldn't drive."). There are also malicious posters who might broadcast this information on their blogs, Facebook pages, or other websites just to hurt someone. It's not libel if it's true, after all. If my children go searching my name on the Internet, what will they find?

The Very Worst Thing
No one was hurt in my accident. My wrecked car could have been the least of my worries in the hours following my arrest. The potential injuries to myself or others are too numerous to list fully. Broken bones, permanent disfigurement, loss of limbs.... My decision to have a few drinks and then driving could have landed me in a hospital just as easily as a jail cell. Me or someone else.

And that's still not the worst thing. Approximately ten thousand deaths a year can be attributed to drunk driving. The deaths of drunk drivers. The deaths of other motorists. The deaths of passengers. The deaths of men and women who just happened to be crossing a street at the wrong time.

I might not have gotten the chance to tell my story. Or I might have been writing it from a prison cell, sentenced for manslaughter or reckless endangerment. I might have killed someone whose only mistake was being in the wrong place at the wrong time. If I hadn't been alone in the car, I could have gotten a coworker killed. Or my wife. Or my children.

It could have been so much worse. If you take nothing else away from my story, take away that I was one of the lucky ones.

Why Companies Should Care
You might be wondering why your employer would invest in this type of message for its employees. You are an adult and probably have done just fine in this area for years. Based on my experience, most people believe they know when they have had enough and when not to get behind the wheel after drinking. They feel that

as long as they are cautious, they can get to where they're going without issues. I certainly did, and look where that got me.

Employers care about their employees, their well-being, and their health. They invest hundreds of thousands of dollars in their people. To lose employees because they were unaware of the consequences of their actions is not a good business decision and only hurts the company both short and long term.

When I heard from human resources to let me know I was fired, it was a five-minute telephone call. From the point of view of the human resources department, it was a matter of weighing the costs of letting me go against the costs of keeping me on as an employee.

The first cost of firing me was the loss of all the time, money, equipment, and personnel involved in training me to do my job. I'd spent eighteen years with this company, and they had spent a tremendous amount of time and money on developing me. My car, phone, computer, health insurance, and retirement benefits were all investments made by the company on the premise of my long-term employment. Everything I'd learned and everything I had to contribute to this organization was gone. On top of that were the time and money spent on letting me go—every decision brings paperwork.

After letting me go, the company then had to find a replacement. That included the cost of recruiting for the position, interviewing, and background checks on the applicants. And once someone was hired, there would be the same training, equipment, benefits package, and moving expenses for that person as there had been for me, this time with the hope that things would turn out better. Of course between the time I was let go and when my replacement was hired, there would be lost productivity and the additional time spent training others to fill in until a permanent replacement could be found. If I had been involved in sales, my dismissal could have resulted in lost customers. If I had been involved in advertising or research, my dismissal could have resulted in lost intellectual property.

Which brings us to why you're reading my story. Firing an employee for drunk driving and keeping an employee who's been convicted of drunk driving are both costly options. The third (and most cost-efficient) option is to prevent the behavior in the first place. The first step is to acknowledge that drunk driving is a very real problem that can shatter the life of any employee regardless of social standing or previous criminal record. The second step is to acknowledge the very real costs that accompany losing and replacing employees (entry-level, senior-level, and all levels in-between). The third step is to address how alcohol is part of our culture, fostered during personal time and by businesses that encourage alcohol consumption at meetings, holiday parties, and special events. Without real life education on the personal and professional liability of failure to change, too many people will continue to make the mistake that I did.

The policy concerning alcohol consumption and driving needs to be more than a subparagraph buried somewhere in the employee handbook. We all need to realize that drinking in moderation, choosing a designated driver, and providing taxi service for employees following company events are safety precautions that are just as essential as protective helmets and "wet floor" signs.

ONE MISTAKE, RELENTLESS PAIN

My nightmare is far from over. I have to manage the completion of my PTI program, work toward the exception to have my probation period reduced and continue meeting the multitude of requirements the probation program requires. In September, I will need to focus on proving I have done what is necessary to re-instate my driver's license.

It has been more than one year since I made the decision to get behind the wheel of a car after drinking too much. That decision has disrupted my career and caused enormous pain and hardship to my family and friends. That one decision has created more anxiety, stress, and embarrassment than I could have imagined. That decision has cost me more than six figures in lost wages, attorney fees, fines, and the list goes on.

I distinctly remember hearing in some driver training class I took a while ago that a DUI would cost $10,000 and potential legal ramifications. I am here to tell you those days are over. I spent $10,000 **within the first month** after being arrested. Potential legal ramifications are **not** potential. They are real, and they sting. Dollars, time, stress, heartache, fear—just a few things that come with it.

I set off to New Jersey with high hopes of a promotion. I ended up broken and broke, confused, frustrated, and tired all because I made one bad decision. We make decisions every day, some big and some small. Please don't make the decision I made. You have just read a firsthand description of what happens when you do.

By the way this story is to be continued. It's not over yet.

Be mindful, careful, and safe.

Authored by a proud father of two perfect kids and husband of the perfect wife of twenty years.

BASIC STATISTICS

- More than 1.5 million people are arrested each year for driving under the influence of alcohol.
- Each year there are more than eleven thousand crash fatalities that involve drivers with blood-alcohol levels of .08 or higher—the average legal limit in the US today.
- There is an active campaign currently in Congress to lower the limit to .05, meaning the odds might get worse for those who roll the dice.
- More than 40 percent of the traffic deaths in the US are alcohol-related.
- Every two minutes someone is injured in an alcohol-related crash.
- Thirty percent of drivers admitted to drinking and driving in the past year.

REALITY

- Alcohol is a part of most corporate cultures. That doesn't mean you can't choose to make wise decisions when it comes to getting into your car after drinking.
- Corporate meetings, team meetings, and customer dinners, just to name a few, are breeding grounds for making bad decisions. I know because I've been there.
- Based on my experience, there are significantly more than 30 percent of people, as listed in the above statistic, who roll the dice. Please don't risk it. It's not worth it.

SELF-REFLECTION GUIDE

1. How often in the last year have you had more than a few drinks and then gotten behind the wheel?
2. Do you know how many beers or drinks it will take **you** to reach the .08 blood alcohol level?
3. Are you aware of your company's policy on DUI or class-one violations?
4. If you were arrested for DUI, how would you explain it to your family and friends?
5. If you lost your job, how would you pay your bills (including legal fees and insurance increases)?
6. What would you do if you could not find a job for twelve months because of a DUI?
7. If you lost your license, how would that affect your life? How would you get around?
8. How would you be affected emotionally dealing with the multitude of issues of a DUI?
9. Do you have a failsafe plan in case you've had too much to drink (a designated driver, the number of a cab company saved on your phone, a friend or spouse who will pick you up)?

For more information visit www.dpkeducation.com
or e-mail the author at dkoch@dpkeducation.com.

Praise for *One Mistake, Relentless Pain*

"*One Mistake, Relentless Pain* is incredibly important on so many fronts. Most employees and companies have no idea of the full ramifications of driving under the influence. Obviously there is a great cost to the employee, but what's lost oftentimes is the tremendous cost to their company. The story is real and resonates on so many levels."
— Jeff D. Tritt, former vice president, People and Culture,
Leo Burnett; chief talent officer, Resource Interactive

"As our culture continues to revolve around alcohol, the need for real and substantive education on the dangers and effects of driving under the influence is critical. *One Mistake, Relentless Pain* is an extremely effective tool not only because it is well written but because it is real and relatable to its audience. This short story will lower corporate costs and, more importantly, save our employees from the pain the author so eloquently describes."
— Jack Darby, president and CEO, Svelte Medical Systems

"*One Mistake, Relentless Pain* does a magnificent job of getting the audience to think and hopefully avoid the financial and emotional pain the author describes. Too many people are uninformed about the true ramifications of driving under the influence. It means tremendous hardship to them and their families but also to their organizations. This is a must-read for all who take that risk."
— Bob Castellini, executive vice president, Morgan Stanley

"This book should be required reading for every company of every size in America. It will definately help save careers and, more importantly, lives."
— Gregg Jackson, national best-selling author,
radio host, and entrepreneur

"Just like corporate America, alcohol is a regular guest at military social functions, and just like corporate America, the military has a low tolerance for any alcohol incident, especially drinking and driving. *One Mistake, Relentless Pain*, although about a civilian's hardship, will hit home and make our men and women think hard about their choices when it comes to drinking and driving. Any unit, chief's mess, or wardroom can learn from Mr. Koch's experiences and with proper leadership implement the lessons he painfully learned so that our service members, who are susceptible to alcohol misuse, don't have to personally repeat this tragedy."
— Captain Todd Lutes, United States Coast Guard